Zoo on the Moon

by David Walker

There's a zoo on the moon,

where no one has been.

It's full of strange creatures

no human has seen.

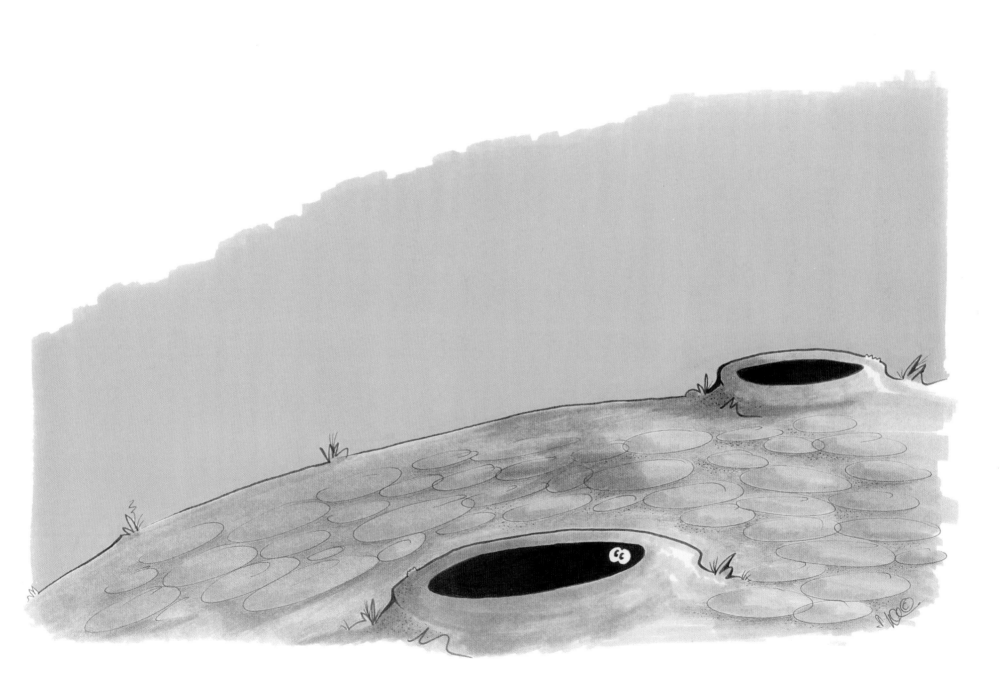

Turtles with false teeth
dangle from trees,
and a great spotted caterpillar
bares knobbly knees.

Elephants have faces
at the end of their tails,
and two-headed penguins
slide along just like snails.

There's a snake with ears
all over its middle,

and giraffes stuck in buckets

do nothing but giggle.

There are crocodile snowmen
with twiglets for hands,

and a down-under ostrich
sticks his head in the sand.

Scuba-diving camels
wear leopard-skin socks,

and sunbathing hot dogs

use mustard sunblock.

Turkeys use chopsticks
and buzzing mice fly,

while two-legged hippos

have only one eye.

There's octopus ice cream,
orangutan pies,

and monkey marshmallows,

with regular fries.

There's an emu with an arm
growing out of its neck,
and invisible hens
that sneak up and peck.

A short-sighted rhino,
with hedgehogs for feet,
tucks up with a book
before going to sleep.

There's a zoo on the moon,
where no human has been.
It's full of strange things
that no one has seen.

But the best thing about it —
it's free to get in;
you just need a rocket ...

... Let the journey begin!

10,9,8,7,6,5,4,3,2,1

Blast off!

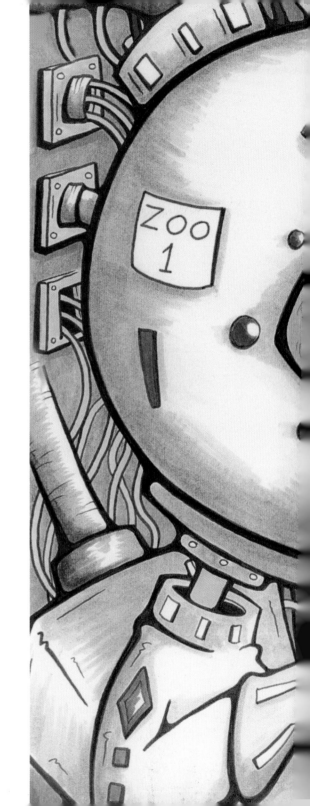

For Freya and George

Published by
Hogs Back Books
34 Long Street
Devizes
Wiltshire SN10 1NT
www.hogsbackbooks.com
Text copyright and illustrations © 2018 David Walker

Printed in Malta
ISBN: 978-1-907432-31-6
British Library Cataloguing-in-Publication Data.
A catalogue record for this book is available from the British Library.
1 3 5 4 2